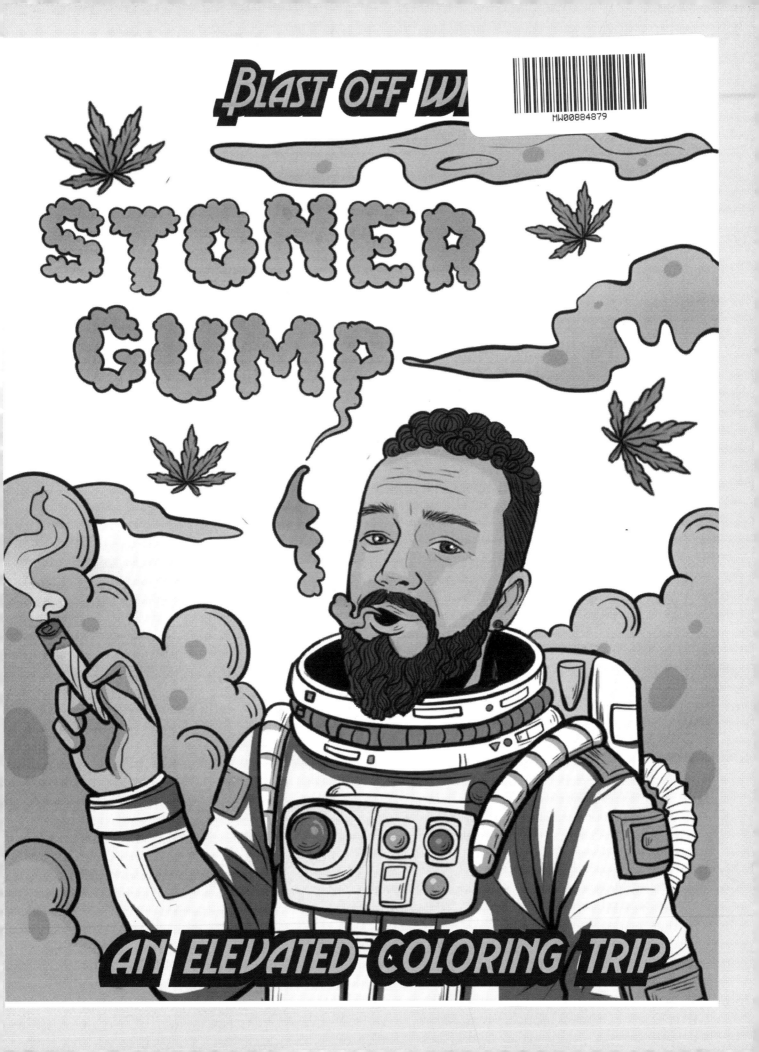

And folks, if you aren't following us - you should be....

StonerGump

Daniel Gossard

Unconventional.mom

Julie Morey

Dedication

Space Cadets and Astronauts
alike, this coloring book was
lovingly made for you.

Fly High Gumplings! And enjloy
this journey through the galaxy!

Thank You!!!

This Book Belongs To

_____

THE CREATOR

Daniel Gossard, known by his online moniker StonerGump, has rapidly captivated a massive audience on TikTok, amassing over a million followers in a remarkably short span. His videos are characterized by a perfect blend of humor and genuine authenticity, making them immensely enjoyable.

Daniel always ensures his audience reaches just the right level of elevation! Whether you're a space cadet or an astronaut, this coloring book promises a delightful journey through space.

And folks, if you are not following him, you should be @stonergump on Tiktok

THE DESIGNER

Julie Morey is a designer with a playful spirit. By day, she is a school social worker, and by night, she crafts whimsical worlds in her three adult coloring books, "The Boozy Unicorn," "The Sassy Mermaid," and "Chicks Gone Wild, as well as numerous journals.

She is excited to team up with StonerGump to bring you a one-of-a-kind playful coloring book, promising a coloring adventure that will tske yoiu to space!

Find her coloring books on Amazon, and follow her @unconventional..mom on TikTok.

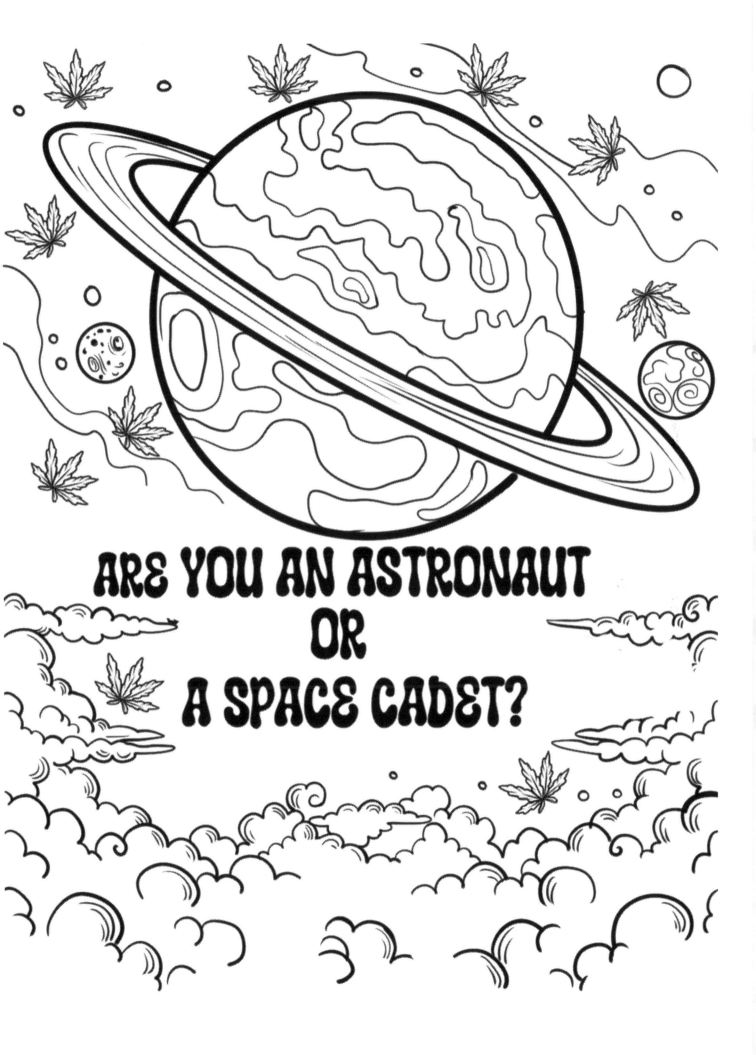

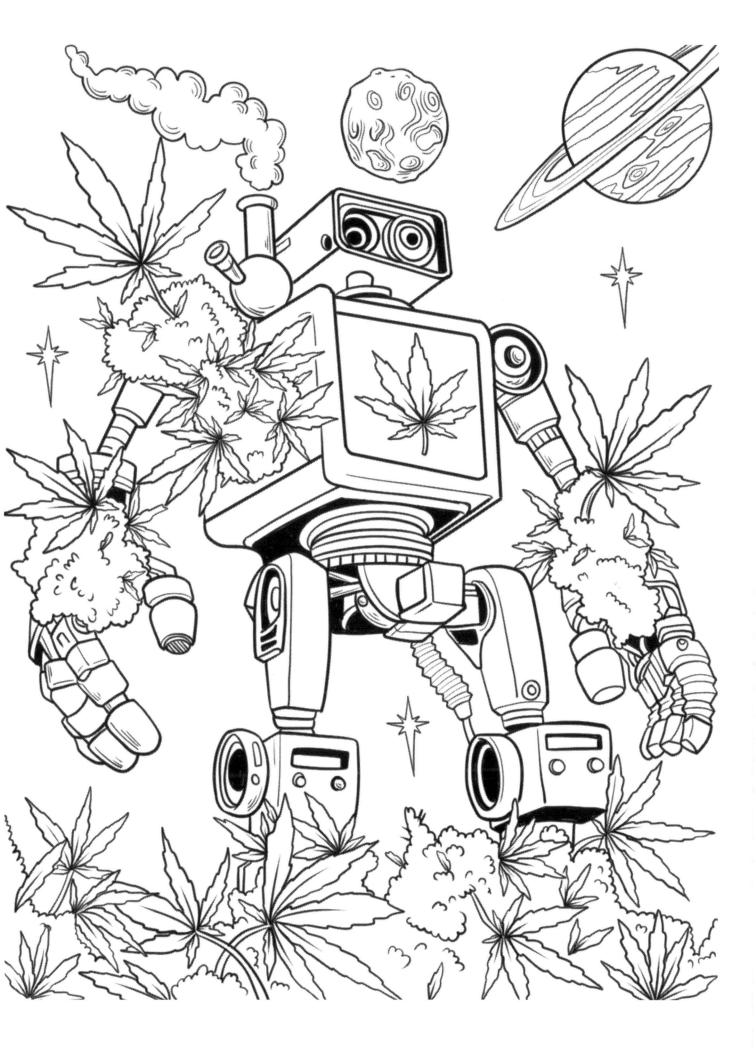

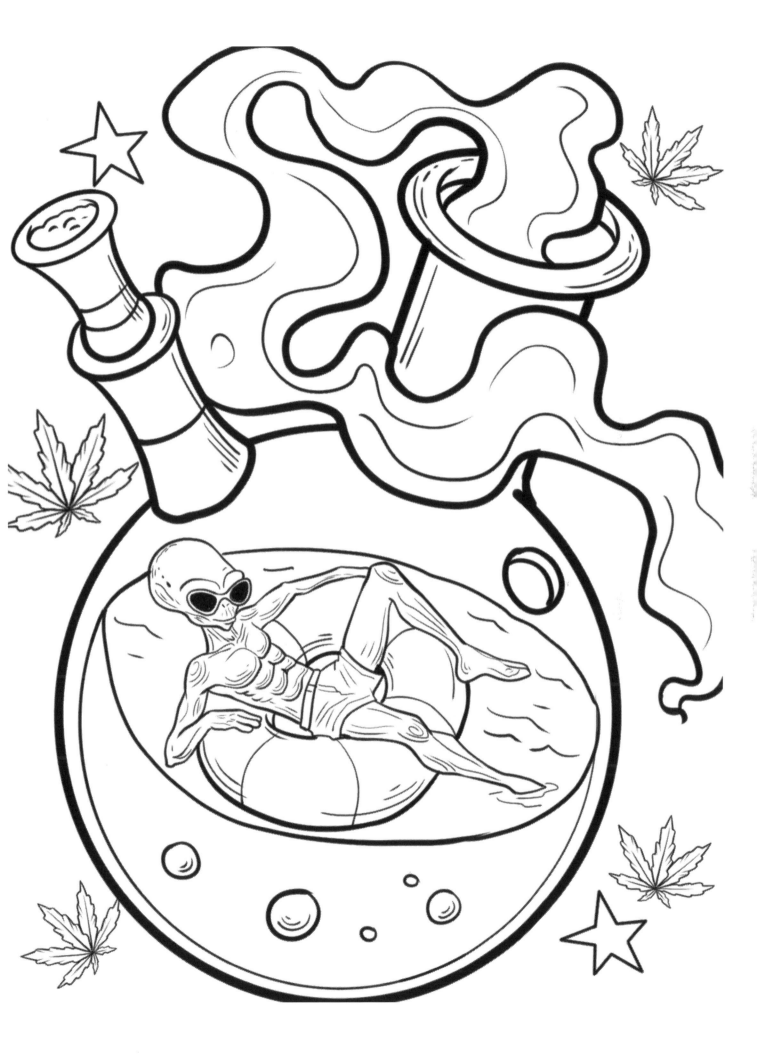

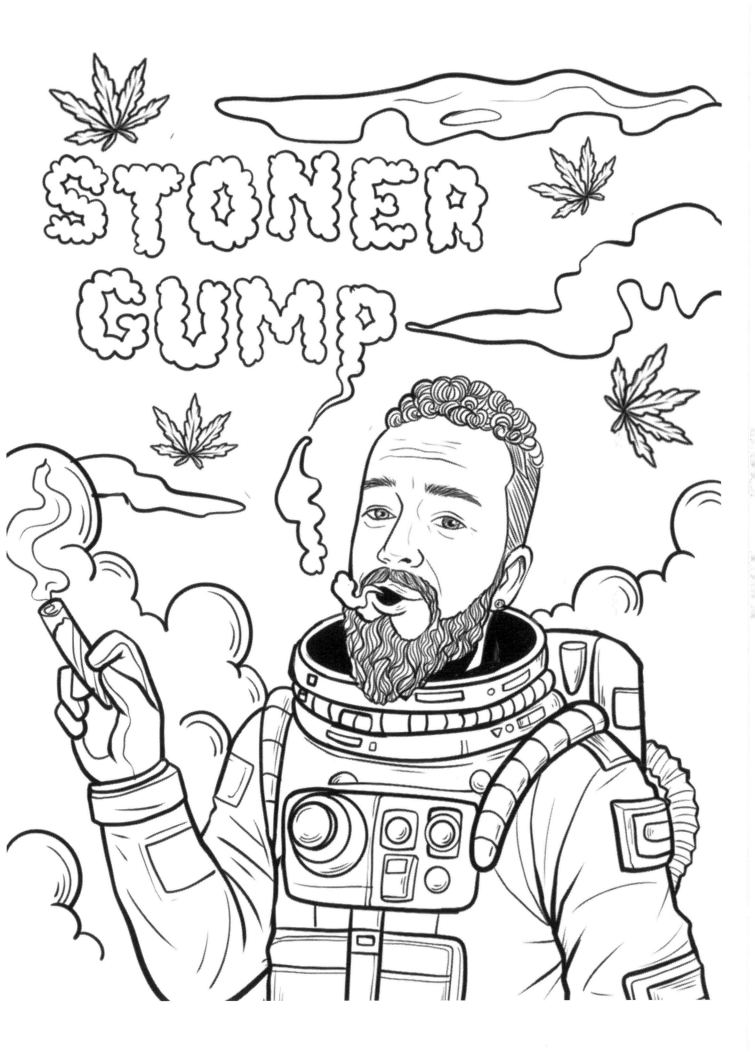

Made in the USA
Columbia, SC
28 August 2024

41248525R00059